Lucille

A BLUEBEARD RETELLING

DAKOTAH GUMM

For Harmony

Without whom this book would never
have been born.

Chapter

The streets are dark and icy as I make my way through the city. Notre Dame looms against the clouds, its twin towers frowning down at me.

"Don't look at me like that," I mutter at the cathedral, tucking my hands deeper into my pockets. "I already know I'm late." If Anne discovers I was out at night, she'll hire a nursemaid to watch over me. She takes her responsibility as head of household seriously.

The thought threatens to suffocate me. My sister is already protective to the extreme. If it wasn't for her nightly work with Les Gardiens, I would never leave her sight, no matter that I'm old enough at twenty-one to make my own decisions.

I'm lucky I've never run into a Gardien during my late-night escapades. Les Gardiens are an elite force of monster hunters, protecting Paris from creatures most people never know exist. If they found out the younger sister of one of their own liked to travel the dark streets of the city, they'd take turns patrolling our home to keep me inside at night.

I stop beneath a burning streetlamp and pull Papa's old watch from the pocket of my coat. Almost half past eleven. Anne usually stops by the house at midnight to check in on me. If I hurry, I can make it.

The cathedral bells chime the half hour, a loud, low warning, as I cross the Seine. I glare up at the towers.

I take a shortcut down a long, narrow alley. Tall homes on either side block the light of the streetlamps, but I don't have time to take the main roads.

Footsteps echo behind me. Glancing back, I see no one, and I hasten my pace. Les Gardiens may protect the city from creatures of evil, but some monsters are human. A thief can be as deadly as a vampire.

The footsteps quicken with mine. My heart catches in my throat. I can see the light of the main road up ahead, but I'm not there yet. The light means safety. Even this late at night, someone is bound to be out. No thief wants to be observed. I just have to reach the road.

My pursuer draws closer, and I break into a run. I'm close now, but so are the steps. I can sense his breath on my neck, feel his hand brush my dress.

I burst out of the alley and onto the main road, skittering to a stop before a tall, well-dressed man.

"Help!" I gasp, doubling over

"Are you in danger, mademoiselle?" He places a hand on my back. "Is someone chasing you?"

I nod, gesturing behind me.

He walks toward the alley. I watch as he disappears into the shadows, returning a moment later.

"I am sorry," he says. "There's no one there."

I've regained my breath, though my heart still beats a furious rhythm. "You must have frightened him off," I say, straightening. "Thank you."

I look up into his face. He's well-dressed in a top hat and overcoat, with a beard so black it looks almost blue by the light of the streetlamp. A threatening aura lurks in his eyes, and I have the sudden, irrational thought that I would have been safer with a thief than with him.

"It's late for a pretty young thing to be out alone," he says. A slight accent marks his words. German, I think. I can't look away from the glint in his dark gray eyes.

"I was on my way home."

"Unaccompanied?" He looks conspicuously around the empty street. "That's unwise. You never know what sort of monsters lurk in the shadows."

I swallow hard. I know all about monsters. After our parents died, Anne ensured I knew all the dangers of our world. Dangers she'd never let me face, keeping me locked away from anything that could cause me harm.

Even after our parents' violent deaths, I'd never given credit to her fears until tonight.

"My show lasted longer than expected," I explain. He holds my gaze, and fear skitters down my spine.

Then he looks away, back toward the alley, and the spell is broken. "Axël?" he asks. "I was at the same show. Did you enjoy it?"

A smile creeps across my face. "It was magnificent. The beauty, the romance—oh! And when they lay there dying in each other's arms!" I clasp my hands to my chest, fear forgotten as I relive the evening. "'Living? Our servants will do that for us,'" I quote, tears pricking at the corner of my eyes. "Wasn't it a sensation?"

He nods solemnly. "Villiers was a master of his art."

We stand there for a moment, looking into each other's eyes. A silent bond connects us. The words we've shared are few, but the understanding between us goes deeper than words. It's a meeting of minds, a joining of souls.

The warning toll of the bells of Notre Dame crash into us, shattering the moment.

I pull out Papa's watch. Quarter to midnight.

"Are you late?"

I groan, slipping the watch back into my pocket. "If I'm not home by midnight, my sister…" I wave my hand in the air. "I have to go."

"Please." He takes my arm. "Allow me to accompany you home. The streets aren't safe at night." He offers a smile, his white teeth glinting in the lamplight.

My heart gives a little flutter in my chest. "Thank you."

There's no time for conversation as we hurry down the streets. We reach the house as the bells chime the hour.

I peek in through the window. All is dark and silent, with no sign of Anne. Relief washes through me. I'm not the only one running late tonight.

"I'll leave you here," my rescuer says as I draw the key from my pocket. "I hope to see you again, Mademoiselle…" He pauses.

"Allard. Lucille Allard."

"Mademoiselle Allard." He flashes a dazzling smile, then takes my hand and kisses the air over it. "Until next time."

My face heats at the attention, and the key slips from my grasp, clattering onto the stone step. I bend to pick it up, saying, "I didn't get your name."

He doesn't respond. When I straighten, he's gone. Frowning, I look up and down the street, but the handsome stranger has vanished.

I stretch my fingers, still feeling the press of his hand through my glove, as I let myself into the house. I've never felt such an instantaneous connection with anyone in my life. He didn't even kiss my hand, just the air over it, but I can feel his lips on my skin. Warmth suffuses my body at the thought, and I close the door behind me, pressing a hand to my heart.

Anne waits for me at the table the next morning, sipping from a silver cup of steaming coffee, when I come down for breakfast. She's wearing her work clothes, the loose black pants offering her the range of motion she needs to fight whatever monsters threaten the city. Her coat hangs over the back of the chair, revealing the dirty white shirt beneath, stained with sweat. She's tossed her belt on the table, its weapons scattered among the breakfast dishes.

"Can't you put your things away before you come to the table?" I wrinkle my nose at the mingling odor of gunpowder and garlic. "It's hard to enjoy breakfast with the stench."

She groans. "Don't start, Lucy."

"Long night?" I pour myself a cup, stirring in several lumps of sugar.

"You have no idea." She leans back in her chair, closing her eyes. "I think there's a new nest in the city. Two bodies in the past week."

"Here?" I ponder the news as I take a drink of the dark, sweet liquid in my cup. The beasts rarely come so far into the city. Whether it's the blessing of the saints of Notre Dame (as Anne claims) or the notoriety of Les Gardiens (as I believe), something about Paris keeps them away.

She scowls out the window. "Not two blocks from Notre Dame. They're getting bolder." She fixes me with a stern look, the patchwork gold-and-cream skin of her face wrinkled with a frown. "You need to be cautious. I'm going to be busy until we find them; I might not have time to check in on you every night. Make sure you're home before the streetlamps are lit, and never go out without protection. I'll reinforce the defenses before I leave tonight."

I frown at one of her "defenses," the noxious purple flowers adorning our windows. I hate them. Garlic is for cooking, not decoration. But I know Anne won't budge on this. It's the same reason an enormous iron cross marks our front door, and all our dishes are pure silver. Ever since she found our parents' bodies in the front hall, drained of blood, she's been cautious to the extreme. Her fear brought her to Les Gardiens, and in the ten years since, she's risen in the ranks, guarding the oblivious inhabitants of Paris from danger.

Anne lets out a heavy sigh and drains the rest of her coffee. "I'm going to bed. I'll see you for supper?" She's the only person I know who can sleep after drinking a full pot of coffee.

"I'll be here," I say, because where else would I be? I have no friends. A social life is impossible to maintain with a curfew before sunset.

"If you do go out, make sure to take Emile." She presses a kiss to the top of my head before leaving the room.

I groan. Emile, our ancient guardian, lives in an apartment in the back of the house. He's half-deaf, half-blind, and completely senile. Most of the time, he forgets Maman and Papa are dead. Our parents left us with a substantial inheritance, enough that we wouldn't have to worry about work or marriage to support ourselves, but living in Paris with money comes with certain…expectations. Anne refuses to let any servants live with us, lest they invite evil into our home. Emile is her one concession to the social conventions around our inheritance. His presence provides a certain respectability to our status, and he doesn't disrupt our lives with expectations we can't fulfill.

I don't want to spend my day dragging Emile around the city, so I go to the drawing room while the day servants clear the breakfast dishes. My paints are where I left them, a fresh canvas waiting. I stretch my fingers, eager to create.

I don't have an image in mind, but I start with a splash of blue. Blacks and purples form around it, creating swirling shadows. Orange lightens the scene as a figure takes shape.

By the time I finish, a face looks up at me from the painting. His dark eyes call to me, a frightening depth in them. They seem to see straight into my soul. It's the man from last night, the one who saved me from whoever was chasing me.

His words echo in my head. You never know what sort of monsters lurk in the shadows. Did he mean that in a general sense? Or does he know about the creatures Les Gardiens fight against? Could he perhaps be one of them?

I shake myself. I'm becoming as suspicious as Anne. Why would a monster warn someone about himself? And he'd saved me. Something—someone—evil wouldn't do that.

I wish I'd gotten his name. He said he hoped to see me again, but he didn't leave his name or any way to contact him. How can I see him again if I don't know who he is?

Maybe he'll be in the same place tonight. If I go back to where he saved me, I can see him again.

Chapter

Anne leaves before dusk, telling me not to wait up. She'll be on the opposite side of the city, too far to check on me. Still, I wait a full hour after the streetlamps are lit before leaving in search of my stranger.

My stranger. It should seem strange, calling him mine, but there's an undeniable connection between us. I'm sure he feels it, too. At least, I hope he does. If I see him tonight, I'll know for sure.

With that optimistic thought, I don my coat and step out into the frigid winter night.

An hour later, I'm beginning to regret my decision to come out tonight. My stranger is nowhere to be seen, and the cold seeps into my bones. I pace the cobbled street, careful to avoid the icy patches. Was I wrong? Didn't he feel the connection between us?

If Anne knew I was out here alone, braving the dangers of the night for a chance to see a strange man, she would never let me leave the house again.

With a heavy sigh, I turn to go.

In my distraction, I don't see the man in front of me before it's too late. I crash into a large body. As I stumble back, powerful arms steady me.

"Out after dark again?" My stranger's hypnotic voice berates me. "I told you it's dangerous."

He releases me, and I shiver as I look up into his face.

"I—" I swallow and try again. "I didn't get to thank you. For yesterday. Saving me."

His brows raise. "Yes, you did, mademoiselle."

Did I? I flush. "Well, I thank you again, then."

He inclines his head in a bow. "The pleasure was mine. But surely you didn't come out tonight just for that?"

My chest tightens. This was foolish of me. "I...wanted to see you again," I admit. "I didn't get your name."

He smiles. "I'm both flattered and concerned that you would risk the dangers of the streets to find out my name, Mademoiselle Allard."

The heat from my face courses through my whole body. "Your name, monsieur?"

"Jakob." He removes his hat—he's once again dressed well, in a top hat and long black coat—and bows with a flourish. "Jakob von Peller."

I curtsey. "Thank you for saving me last night, Monsieur von Peller."

"Now that the social niceties have been observed, might I escort you home?" His smile mocks me. "Or did you have plans?"

My heartbeat quickens. "I'm not expected anywhere. I'd..." I trail off, suddenly shy. No, it's too late for that. I raise my chin, meeting his gaze. "I'd hoped to spend some time with you. To get to know you better, monsieur."

Emotion flashes through his eyes, too quick to identify. Then he offers me his arm. "I was on my way to a cabaret. I would be honored if you would join me."

I can't help the grin that lights up my face. I straighten my coat, glad I dressed well. My gown is simple but nice enough for an evening out, a deep blue with puffed shoulders and tight sleeves. I piled my golden hair on top of my head and pinned it there, leaving loose curls cascading down my back, and I even added a touch of powder to my face, lightening my already pale skin and turning my cheeks pink.

A scant dusting of snow begins to fall, lending a romantic atmosphere to the night. "You're not French," I observe as we walk. "What brings you to Paris?"

"I'm visiting…family," he says. "It's a trip I've been putting off for some time."

"Does your family live here?" Perhaps I've met them. I long to know more about him, this man who calls to my soul.

"For the moment." An ironic smile touches his lips. "They're…itinerant. Yours lives here, though, do they not?"

I nod. "My sister. Our parents were killed when I was a child. Anne works late hours, so I'm alone a lot." I realize the impression my words must give, and I stutter. "Not that she's—she's not a—Her work is respectable!"

He glances at me. "I would never dare to assume otherwise. Your sister is your protector, is she not?"

Protector. An odd word choice. Does he know about Les Gardiens, the work Anne does protecting the city? But how could he? "Yes," I answer. "She's been my guardian since our parents died."

"I imagine she disapproves of your late-night wanderings. She must know the dangers that roam the streets."

My skin prickles at the reminder of last night. I draw closer to Jakob, glad he's with me. Something deep in my soul assures me he wouldn't hurt me.

"She's overprotective," I say. "But I'm safe with you."

He stops walking, and the smile he gives me is sharp. "No one else can threaten you while you are with me."

There's an undertone in his words that sends a chill down my spine, but before I can think it through, he gestures at a club across the street.

We're in a part of town I've never explored, but I've heard of the place he's brought me. It's Le Cabaret de l'Enfer—the Cabaret of Hell. A monstrous, gaping maw marks the entrance; hellish orange light and deep organ music pour out from the barred windows. Demons and their victims adorn the outer walls.

A man dressed as the devil stands at the entrance. He wears a tight red suit, a black cape, and a grotesque horned mask. A pair of men in eveningwear approach. "Enter and be damned," he tells them, his voice echoing across the street.

I shiver, looking up at Jakob. Half his face, cast in shadow, is pallid, his beard black with a tinge of blue. Light from the cabaret dances across the other half of his face, transforming him into an inhabitant of hell.

"Are you frightened, mademoiselle?" He raises a brow in question.

Terrified. But I can't deny I'm intrigued. And hasn't he promised I'm safe with him? "I trust you," I say, tightening my grip on his arm.

"The more fool you." He doesn't give me another chance to walk away, though, before guiding me across the street toward the cabaret.

The devilish doorman takes Jakob's ticket, leering at me through the holes in his mask.

"She's my guest," Jakob says.

"Welcome to l'Enfer," the doorman says with a wicked cackle. "Enter, and be damned!"

The inside of the building is even more gruesome than the outside. Horrifying statues reach down from the low ceiling, grasping at the inhabitants around the tables. On a small stage, a half-naked man addresses the crowd, a pitchfork in his hand and his bare chest painted with swirls of black and red. On the front wall, next to the door, someone plays an onyx organ, the strains a menacing accompaniment to the speaker's monologue.

Despite the macabre atmosphere, the crowd is raucous, laughing at something the man on stage said. Jakob leads me past the stage to a booth in the back of the room and takes a seat next to me. I lean into him, giving the decorated ceiling a wary look.

"Coffee for both of us," Jakob tells the waitress that approaches. "With cognac in mine."

"Cognac in both," I correct. I've never had cognac, but I'll need the extra courage. The surroundings have me on edge, though I would never admit it aloud.

The waitress slips away, but another woman takes her place. She wears a scandalously low ballgown, and her scarlet lips form a pout as she slides into the booth across from Jakob. She places a gloved hand on his arm. "I was wondering where you were, Jakob, darling." She gives me an appraising look and bares her teeth in an approximation of a smile. "But you brought a friend! How marvelous."

He removes her hand, fixing her with a glare. "Leave her alone, Leda. She is with me."

She twists a sable curl around her finger, taking a sip of the sickly green liquid in her cup. "Ah, yes. I'd forgotten you don't like to share."

Share? She's talking about me like a meal. The hairs on my arms raise. Jakob, I trust—though reason insists I shouldn't—but this woman sets my teeth on edge. I feel as though I'm trapped in a booth with a predator, and she's deciding how best to pounce.

Have I stumbled into the clutches of a vampire? And if I have, why does Jakob associate with her? Does he not know what she is?

The waitress returns with our coffees, heedless of the tension at the table. I take a large drink of mine, the bitter liquid scorching my tongue. I cough as the heat and alcohol burn down my throat.

Jakob loops his arm around my waist, drawing me closer, and speaks low in my ear. "As I told you, Mademoiselle Allard, you have nothing to fear from others as long as you are with me. I promise you will return home unmolested by morning."

The words combine with the alcohol to soothe my frazzled nerves. "Lucille," I say. It seems foolish for him to call me "mademoiselle" while we sit in such an intimate manner. "Call me Lucille."

"Lucille." My name slips from his mouth like a prayer. His gaze drops to my lips, and I part them, my breath catching in my throat.

His friend coughs, and he scowls, turning back to her.

"Aren't you going to introduce me?" she asks.

With a heavy sigh, Jakob says, "Leda, this is Lucille Allard. Lucille, Leda is my…sister."

"It's nice to meet you," I murmur. His sister? The way she looks at him is far from familial. Jealousy strikes me between the ribs, and I bite my lip to keep from frowning.

"A delight." She raises her glass to me, flashing another smile that shows all her teeth. Then she turns back to Jakob. "I hope you'll accept Aeron's proposal. We've missed you."

"I've made my thoughts on that clear." Jakob's voice is almost a growl.

I wonder what proposal this Aeron could have made, to provoke such a response.

"Come, now, dear Jakob." A man's honey-sweet voice cuts through the chatter of the club and the chords of the organ. I look up to see an olive-skinned man smiling down at us. "You bring a

unique perspective. Your taste for beauty is unpar-
alleled. What good are your talents if you won't
use them to benefit the family?"

"What benefits does the family bring me?"
Jakob asks as the man slides into the booth next to
Leda, whose toothy smile is even wider now.

"Companionship," he says, waving for the waitress. "Protection."

"I can protect myself, as you know, and
I do not desire the type of…companionship
you provide."

The newcomer turns his attention from Jakob
to me. "We are remiss to neglect such a lovely crea-
ture. I am Aeron." He reaches across the table and
snatches my hand, raising it to his lips. My skin
crawls at the touch, but I don't pull away.

"Aeron is the man who fathered me," Jakob
says, his mouth tightening. "Aeron, this is Lucille Allard."

His father? There's no familial resemblance,
and this man seems no older than Jakob, who can't
be above thirty himself. It seems impossible to believe that Aeron fathered him. Judging by appear-
ances, I would place Leda as the oldest of the three,
at about thirty-five. But what reason would Jakob
have to lie to me?

"Allard?" Aeron asks, his eyes narrowing. I lick my lips, nervous, as I nod. "What a beautiful name. Do you have any relations?"

"A sister," I mutter, inching closer to Jakob. There's no room between us, but he tightens his arm around me. He promised me I would return home safe tonight. I have to remember that.

Aeron sits back, the suspicious look gone in a blink. "Then you must understand the importance of family. Jakob, the dear boy, does not. He insists on living alone in that godforsaken castle in Alsace, or traveling in solitude. Tell me, what is life without companionship?"

"I find sufficient companionship without your assistance," Jakob says.

I shift in my seat, uncomfortable. Does he mean other women? It's foolish for me to be jealous, I know, but I can't help the pang that pierces my chest. I've known him for a single day, but I don't want to share him with anyone else.

"You do find the most beautiful friends." Aeron nods at me in acknowledgment.

My sense of discomfort rises, and I take a drink of my coffee to avoid looking into his disconcerting brown eyes. The coffee has cooled some, but the temperature does nothing for the taste. If anything, it's even worse now, sharp and bitter. I continue drinking, anxious to avoid Aeron's gaze.

After a beat of silence at the table, broken up by the fiddles and the jeering crowd, Aeron continues. "But even the beauty of your playmates can't compare to the bond of family."

Playmates? The word sinks in my stomach. I thought the connection I have with Jakob was special, but maybe I'm just one in a long line of women.

"Did you have something new to say, Aeron, or did you come to reiterate the same tired argument?" Jakob's gaze wanders around the cabaret. He takes a sip of his coffee before looking back at his father.

Their relationship is unconventional; I would never have called Papa by his first name, nor dared to speak to him in such a manner. The mystery fuels my desire to know more about Jakob and his strange family.

"I will change my argument when you change your reply, dear Jakob."

"Then there is nothing more to discuss." Jakob stands, extending a hand to me. I set down my now-empty coffee cup and allow him to help me to my feet. I feel warm, sort of fuzzy, and the room seems brighter and louder than before. It's a reaction to the cognac, I assume. I've never had anything stronger than wine, my intake—like everything in my life—carefully monitored by Anne.

Jakob tucks my arm into his and bows his head to Leda and Aeron. "I will see you in the morning," he says before guiding me out of the club.

Once we're out on the street, his grip on my arm loosens. "I apologize for my family," he says. "They do not always understand the effects their behaviors have on others."

"I'm glad I met them." Despite my discomfort, it feels like I've gleaned insight into Jakob's character, small though that insight may be. "I'd like you to meet my sister, too."

He laughs, the sound grim. "I do not think your sister would like me."

He's right. She suspects anyone she doesn't already know, and especially anyone from outside the city. "But I do," I say, emboldened by the warmth running through my veins. "She'll have to like you once she sees I do."

He stops, turning to me with a stern expression. "I fear you may misunderstand my character, Lucille. I am not a good man."

I feel that same prickle I'd noticed last night when we met. He's dangerous, and some ancient instinct urges me to run.

But just like last night, I'm compelled to lean closer. I look into his gray eyes, and my breath hitches, cheeks flooding with heat.

He notices, and his mouth turns up at the corner. "You should not trust me," he says, his voice low, seductive. He places his hand on my waist and draws me closer.

"But I do." I put my hand on his chest, turning my head up and parting my lips for him.

In answer, he ducks his head to brush his lips over mine. His kiss is soft, his skin cold. Or maybe I'm warm, flushed from emotion and alcohol. Heat pools low in my abdomen, a pulsing sensation stronger than I've ever felt before.

I want to deepen the kiss, to draw closer and explore these new feelings, but he pulls back. "It is late. I should see you home before your sister returns."

I nod, my breath ragged from our kiss—from my first kiss. My thoughts swirl so fast I can't distinguish them from one another.

At the door, he stops and takes my hand. "I would like to see you again. Will you meet me tomorrow after the lamps are lit? There, at the end of the street." He points to a lamppost. "No more wandering the streets alone at night," he adds with a crooked smile.

My heart flutters in my chest. My throat is too tight to form words, so I nod instead. He squeezes my fingers, then swoops down to kiss me again. This kiss is firmer, more substantial, but I have no time to process it before he releases me.

"Good night, my dear Lucille. Until tomorrow."

Chapter

I wake late in the afternoon to a knock and the murmur of voices at the front door. Footsteps follow, and someone knocks on Anne's door. A few minutes later, I hear the thump of my sister's boots on the hallway floor. The front door opens, then slams shut.

I wrap myself in a dressing gown and go downstairs to find our ancient guardian sitting at the supper table, reading a newspaper.

"Good afternoon, Emile," I say, sitting across from him. I pour myself a cup of coffee and make a face. It's cold—no surprise, since it's probably left over from this morning.

"Where have you been all day, ma chérie?" Emile scolds. He frowns, but the endearment takes the sting from his tone and expression.

"I couldn't sleep last night." It's not a lie. It would have been difficult to sleep in the Cabaret de l'Enfer. "I slept late today."

His mustache twitches as he considers me. "Sleeping the whole day away. What will your father think?" Tsking, he goes back to his paper. "You can explain to him yourself. I won't be making excuses for you."

"Yes, Emile." I sigh. It's easier to humor him than to explain when he forgets about Maman and Papa.

The day maid brings in a dish of beef bourguignon, a stew made from vegetables, red wine, and leftover meat from yesterday's roast. I wrinkle my nose as she leaves, reaching instead for the crusty bread on the table. It's too early for such a heavy meal.

I slather a chunk of the bread in sweet yellow butter and take a bite, leaning over my plate to prevent dropping crumbs all over my dressing gown. "Where is Anne?"

He folds his paper and sets it aside, ladling himself a bowl of stew. "She left for the evening. Dressed in trousers, I might add. Trousers!" Giving a pointed look at my appearance, he adds, "I thought I taught you girls better, but neither one of you has any sense of propriety."

Abashed, I remove my elbows from where they rest on the table and set my bread on the plate. "I'm sorry, Emile," I say, mustering my sweetest smile. "You know we don't mean anything by it."

"Yes, well." His eyebrows come together, but he reaches over to pat my hand. "These past few years have been difficult for you, I know. You need a woman's guiding touch."

He's lucid, at least for the moment. I shrug. "We're managing." I don't want another woman controlling my life; Anne does enough of that on her own. I miss my mother, but Anne has stepped into her role in my life. No, the one I miss the most is Papa.

My chest tightens. Even though it's been years since their deaths, I can picture Papa as though it was yesterday. I smell his pipe tobacco wafting through the air, see the twinkle in his eye as he tells some joke.

Emile is a poor substitute, though I know he tries his hardest. He bears a passing resemblance to Papa, the distant relationship—he's a third cousin twice removed, or something of that sort—apparent in the hooked nose and the swirl on the crown of his head, but aside from that, they're nothing alike. Papa was warm

and jovial, where Emile, though no less af-
fectionate, is old-fashioned and stern. If Papa
had caught me wearing a dressing gown and
sitting with my elbows on the table, he would
have laughed and brushed the crumbs from my
chin, not scolded me for it.

I push the memories away as I rise from the
table. "I'm going out this evening."

"Out again?" He reaches for his paper
again, muttering to himself about, "Young people these days."

Upstairs, I search through my wardrobe for
the perfect dress. Tonight is my first official
outing with Jakob—the first planned outing—
and I want to look my best.

I settle on a cobalt velvet gown embroi-
dered with champagne-colored chrysanthemums. Curling my hair in tight ringlets, I
pin it low in the back and finish it off with a
black feathered ornament that brings out the
darker shades in my golden hair. As I consid-
er myself in the mirror, I add a sapphire and
gold necklace and matching earrings. The
blue of the gemstones matches my eyes, and I
grin, giddy with excitement for whatever the
night may bring.

It's almost seven when I grab my coat from
its hook by the front door and slip out into the
cold. The night is clear, the moonlight bright

as day. I stop on the step and take a deep breath of the crisp air.

Glancing down the street, I see Jakob waiting for me. My heart skips a beat, and I walk toward him, trying not to rush.

"You look lovely tonight, my dear Lucille." He takes my gloved hand and presses a kiss to it. Heat spreads from his lips throughout my whole body.

"Where are we going?" I ask, breathless, as he tucks my arm in his and leads me down the street.

"I have a private box at the opera." He looks sideways at me. "You enjoy opera, do you not?"

"Yes!" My experiences are slim. Anne doesn't approve of most theater performances, and she's too busy with Les Gardiens to take me out at night. Still, I enjoyed the few operas I've seen.

We walk in companionable silence until we reach the opera house. I've only seen the Palais Garnier from the street, but it's magnificent. Electric light streams from the doors and windows. Crowds of lavishly dressed men and women mill around, the chatter of their conversation filling the air. Even in one of my best dresses, I feel almost shabby amid all of the opulence.

Inside, the beauty is staggering. I look around, eyes wide, but there's too much to see. An enormous white marble staircase rises before us. Everything is gilded, and paintings and statues of gods and cherubs adorn the walls and ceiling.

"Impressive, is it not?" Jakob has to lean close to make his voice heard over the crowd. His breath, cool compared to the heated air around us, sends a shiver through me.

"It's—" I shake my head, unable to form words. I've seen beauty before; Paris well deserves its reputation as the most beautiful city in the world. But this opera, new though it may be when compared to wonders such as Notre-Dame and the Musée du Louvre, is unlike anything I've ever seen.

"You are speechless." Jakob squeezes my hand. "I understand."

I try to take it all in as we make our way up the grand staircase and toward the theater. At our box, a valet takes our coats as I look around.

Red velvet covers every surface in the small room. A curtain separates the door and coat rack from the six cushioned chairs on the balcony. I run my hand over the wooden frame of a chair and take a deep breath of the warm, perfumed air.

"Wine?"

"Yes, please." I turn to look at Jakob, who's holding two glasses of red wine. Now that he's taken off his overcoat, I can see the suit he's wearing. It's black, the tails fashionably long, and the waistcoat beneath is a deep burgundy. The dark fabric of his trousers clings to his legs, hinting at strong muscles. What do they look like without the cloth trapping them? My tongue darts out to wet my lips.

He notices me staring and quirks his mouth in a smile.

I cough, embarrassed, and take the offered glass. "Thank you."

The lights dim as the orchestra begins the opening strains of a low, haunting melody. Jakob gestures for me to sit, and he takes the chair next to me, his knee brushing mine.

A rush of cold air announces an arrival in the box. A moment later, the curtain opens, and Jakob's sister walks in, hanging on the arm of a disheveled looking gentleman.

"Oh!" she says, catching sight of us. "I didn't know you were coming tonight, dear Jakob."

His eyes narrow. "I could say the same to you."

She ignores his apparent displeasure, fixing me with a wide smile. "Mademoiselle Lucille! How wonderful to see you again." She guides her companion to a seat, then perches on his lap, draping an arm around his neck. "This is wonderful, the four of us together like this."

The man she's with doesn't speak. I don't smell alcohol, aside from my wine, but he looks intoxicated. He watches Leda through heavy-lidded eyes, jaw slack. He's pale, and there's a red-brown stain on his shirt collar.

Jakob glares at his sister, then tucks his arm around me before settling back in his seat. I do my best to focus on the opera below as a chorus of grim-looking Hebrews sing a prayer for deliverance. The show is Samson et Dalila. A Bible story. Even Anne can't object to this, though she would certainly object to my companions.

I glance at Leda, who's wearing a gown of deep orange and gold. She takes hold of the double string of pearls around her neck and trails them down her man's chest. He tightens his grip on her waist, and she grins, baring her teeth at him.

Clearing my throat, I turn my attention back to the stage, but my mind remains on the couple sitting near us. They're so wrapped up in each other, nothing else matters. He's intoxicated, but I don't think alcohol has anything to do with it. He's intoxicated by her, hypnotized by her very presence. There's no barrier of modesty between them. It's as though they're alone in the theater.

Part of me longs for that, to lose my inhibitions and wrap myself up in Jakob. My breath comes faster, skin growing hot as I allow myself to picture it. I could climb onto his lap and pepper his face and neck with kisses. He would grab me by the waist and hold me tight enough to bruise, matching my kisses with his own.

Looking up, I see him watching me, his eyes hooded with desire. Can he sense my thoughts somehow? Or does he feel the same pull that I feel toward him?

He leans in to whisper something in my ear, and I melt at the nearness.

"I'd hoped for a more private evening for us, my dear Lucille."

I give him a wry smile. "Me, too," I whisper.

"Would you like to leave? I'm certain we can find better entertainment elsewhere."

There's a low, seductive tone to his words that sets every nerve in my body tingling. I bite my lip, nodding, and we leave the box, unnoticed by Leda and her paramour.

Back outside, the cold air does nothing to relieve the heat rushing through me. Jakob flags down a passing taxi and bundles me inside, saying something to the driver that I don't hear before he climbs in behind me.

The air inside the carriage is thick with tension. Neither one of us dare to speak. It's as if words will break the fragile hold we have on ourselves, and we'll crash into each other, inexorably drawn by this magnetism between us.

It feels like hours before the carriage stops, though I know it can only have been minutes. Jakob helps me out, and I look around the street at our destination.

We're standing in front of the library. This late at night, it's closed, all within dark and silent.

I frown up at him, but he presses a finger to his lips, watching as the taxi drives away.

Once we're alone on the street, he leads me to the door. I expect it to be locked, but it opens for him, and we step into the silent building.

This time of day, everything looks different. The moon sends streams of light through the circular windows in the ceiling, casting odd shadows on the stacks of books filling the enormous room.

Jakob leads me to the centermost pool of moonlight. Slowly, he removes my coat, then his own, and spreads them on the floor.

"Jakob—" Before I can say anything else, his lips crash into mine.

I give in to his touch, twining my arms around his neck and deepening the kiss. He tastes rich and bitter, like the merlot wine we were drinking earlier. His hands roam my body, exploring my curves through the fabric of my dress.

He lays me down on top of our coats and trails kisses down my body, over my dress. I whimper, tangling my hands in his hair to keep from writhing. He kisses back up, stopping at my neck. "My sweet Lucille," he murmurs against my skin. "I want you."

The heat between my legs grows, and I take his face in my hands. "Jakob..." I whisper his name.

"Tell me you want me, too." He continues his exploration up my bare leg.

I shouldn't. I've never done anything like this before. Never even kissed a man until I met him. But I can't resist the sensations building inside me. "I do." I nod frantically. "I want you, Jakob."

I expect him to take me then—I'm not entirely uneducated on the act of intercourse—but he kisses down my body until he reaches my center. He kisses me there, and moisture floods in the wake of his tongue. He takes the nub between my legs into his mouth and sucks on it. Gripping my dress in tight fists, I bite back a moan.

What am I doing? We're here in the middle of the library where anyone could see us, and I'm letting a man I barely know kiss and lick between my legs. On his knees before me, Jakob's hair glows blue in the white moonlight. The air smells of old books and desire, and the sound of our breaths fills the air.

My pleasure grows, rising in an unstoppable wave. As it crests, I feel a sharp pain. I cry out, the sound echoing throughout the empty room, but the pain fades in an instant. I'm lost in the tide of sensations. Jakob drinks me up, tongue lapping at my center, until I tug at his hair.

"No more," I beg. I'm boneless, unable to take another moment.

He crawls up my body, licking his lips. "You taste like salvation."

I want to flush, but I can't find the energy. I feel drained, lightheaded and exhausted. Jakob lifts me up and sets me on a table, smoothing my dress back down my legs.

"That wasn't..." I struggle to gather my thoughts. I'm cold, and my mind is in a fog. "I didn't expect it to be like that."

He smiles, wrapping my coat around me. "It was everything, my sweet Lucille."

"But you didn't—" Frowning, I gesture at his body. He claimed to want me, but he didn't complete the act. "We didn't..." I hope he understands what I mean. My eyelids are heavy, drooping.

"Your pleasure is enough to sate my desire." He places his coat over my shoulders, on top of my own, and lifts me into his arms, holding me close to his chest.

The words fill me with comfort that reaches down to my bones. I curl into him, closing my eyes, and oblivion claims me.

When I open them again, we're standing outside my house. I blink up at the enormous iron cross on the door.

Jakob sets me gently on my feet. "How are you feeling?" he asks, brushing a hair from my face.

"Dizzy." The world swims around me, and I cling to his arm. "Will you come inside?" I don't trust myself to make it up the stairs without assistance.

His eyes widen a fraction, but he nods. "Of course."

It takes me a few tries to get the key into the lock, but Jakob is patient with me. He lets me open the door, a steadying arm around my waist. He guides me inside, through the foyer and into the sitting room, where he settles me on the velvet chaise longue.

"You need something to revive you," he says as he lights the lamp. "I'll make you some tea."

Once he disappears through the opposite door, I lie down and close my eyes. He rouses me a few minutes later with a steaming cup of red tea.

Jakob helps me sit up, wrapping my hands around the small china teacup. I wonder for a moment where he found it. All our dishes are silver, save for the iron pots and pans. "Drink."

I take a drink. It's raspberry leaf, flavored with honey and lemon. Jakob observes me, ensuring I finish it. Once the cup is empty, he refills it from the iron teapot on the table and hands me a plate of dried fruits and crackers. "Eat."

I pick up a prune and nibble on it. Already I'm feeling better, the bone-deep cold I felt chased away by the warmth of the tea.

"I'm sorry if I ruined the evening," I say. I don't know why our interlude in the library left me feeling so drained. I'm not prone to fainting spells, and our activities weren't vigorous enough to cause such exhaustion. Surely this isn't what love-making is like all the time?

"You ruined nothing." Jakob cups my face in his hands, skin still chilled from the winter night outside. "I asked too much of you tonight."

I shiver from his touch, and he smiles. "Eat," he repeats before going to light a fire.

After a few minutes, I'm warm enough to shed the coats. Jakob sits next to me on the couch and removes the pins from my hair, combing it out with gentle hands. His soft touch and the warmth of the crackling fire lull me into a contented torpor, and I close my eyes, leaning back against him. I could spend the rest of my life like this.

Chapter 4

I wake the next morning in my own room. I'm dressed in my long ivory nightgown, my hair loose across the pillow. Sunlight streams through the window, illuminating a bouquet of white chrysanthemums in a vase on my dresser.

A smile spreads across my face, and I slide out from beneath the quilts and pad over to the dresser. My mind flashes through the events of last night, from the opera to the library to the drawing room downstairs. I'll never be able to see any of those places again without thinking of Jakob.

I gather the flowers he left for me in my hands and raise them to my nose. They're not sweet-smelling, like roses or lilies, but I love the earthy scent.

Next to the vase is a note written in large, graceful letters. Have dinner with me tonight, my sweet Lucille. Meet me outside at seven o'clock.

My grin widens, and I fold the paper and tuck it beneath my pillow. The day ahead promises to be long and boring, but I'll see Jakob tonight. I can hardly wait.

Jakob and I explore the city together every night after that. He shows me parts of Paris I've never seen before, leading me down streets Anne would never let me near, and though some of them are less than safe, I'm secure with Jakob at my side. He won't allow anyone to threaten me.

Some nights are simple, and we sit on a bench by the river, too engaged in conversation to note the cold or the passing of time. He often returns me home in the early hours of the morning, when the stars have disappeared but the sky hasn't quite begun to lighten. We part on the doorstep with a sweet kiss that lingers on my lips throughout the day, and I find myself imagining a future with him. We've known each other for a couple brief weeks, but I've fallen in love with him.

Tonight we wander through the Musée du Louvre, and Jakob tells me about the art in stories so vivid, it's as if he was there. As we look at paintings by Rembrandt, he talks about his Dutch adventures, intermingling descriptions of rivers and dikes with scandalous histories of Rembrandt's lavish lifestyle and numerous affairs.

In one room, a painting titled The Triumph of Marie de' Medici decorates the ceiling, and Jakob describes for me the Cathedral of Santa Maria del Fiore, where Maria de Medici's proxy wedding was held. I feel as though I'm standing within the cathedral dome myself, looking up at the bright colored scenes of angels and saints.

After hours in the museum, we go to dinner. Jakob orders foie gras and expensive wine for both of us, and while we wait for our food, he takes my hands.

"Are you enjoying the evening?" he asks.

"It's perfect." I'd seen most of the art before—the Louvre is one of the few outings Anne approves of—but Jakob's commentary made the experience so much richer. "I loved hearing about your travels. I've always wanted to see the world."

"Where would you like most to go?"

I think about it. "Egypt."

"The pyramids." His mouth turns up at the corner. "They are impressive."

"You've seen them? What are they like?" Envy burns through me.

"Enormous. From a distance, they almost blend in with the landscape, but closer up, you can see the stones they're made of, massive blocks of sandstone standing almost as tall as I am and weighing over two tons each. On a clear night, with a full moon, it's bright enough to climb to the top."

I'm breathless, picturing the scene. "What does it look like from the top?" I whisper.

"The whole world stretches out before you." His eyes go distant. "Moonlight paints the world gray, and the silver Nile snakes through the land. To one side, you can see Cairo, the lamps of the city flickering orange, and to the other—pure wilderness. Wild camels rest on the sand, and an owl swoops through the sky, searching for prey. Below you, the Sphinx sits in her silent vigil, watching over the desert."

"Here you are, monsieur."

The voice of the server shatters the image in my mind. Blinking, I look around, and the room comes back into focus. This late at night, we're the only guests, and the dim lighting of the ornate dining room enhances the sense of intimacy. I'd almost forgotten we were in public.

The server sets our plates before us and pours us each a glass of sweet Sauternes wine, then disappears. Jakob raises his glass to me.

"To my sweet Lucille," he says, the low tone of his voice sending a rush of heat through me. "May you see the world."

I take a large swallow of the wine to hide my emotion. For a few minutes, we're silent as we eat. The foie gras is delicious, smooth and buttery, but I can't focus on the food. There's a burning in Jakob's eyes that promises an encore to our previous performance in the library. Though we've kissed since then, Jakob has been the consummate gentleman, and the extended abstinence has me desperate for his touch. Desire coils low in my stomach, and I squeeze my legs together, willing myself to look away.

"Where else have you traveled?" I ask, hoping conversation will distract from the tension burning between us, at least until our dinner is done.

A humorous smile touches his lips. "The better question would be where have I not traveled?"

I raise my brows. "India?"

He nods.

"China?"

Another nod.

"America?"

"I spent a year exploring the country."

My jaw nearly drops to the table. He's traveled more than one person should be able to in a single lifetime. I want to hear everything he's seen. "What was your favorite destination?"

His brow creases as he considers my question, but a sound at the door makes us both look up.

Aeron strides in, an agitated scowl on his brown face. He looks around the room, mouth tightening further when he sees us.

"Please excuse me," Jakob says, rising and dropping his napkin on the table. He strides across the room toward his father.

Dread gnaws in my stomach. The room seems to have grown colder, and I wrap my scarf tighter around me. In the doorway, Aeron speaks, the words hushed so I can't hear. Jakob's eyes widen with surprise, then settle into a mask of anger. I shiver at the sight, his beautiful features contorted with rage. At who, I wonder?

He says something in response to Aeron, who nods once before leaving.

Jakob takes a moment to compose himself, then walks back across the room to me, his expression somber but no longer furious.

"Forgive me, Lucille, but I must cut our evening short."

I rise, reaching for his hand. "Is something wrong?"

"Nothing to concern you." He shakes his head. "My foolish sister has gotten herself into trouble. Aeron would like my assistance in rectifying the situation."

"Oh." I'm disappointed, but at least it's not something more serious—like his father's disapproval of our relationship. "If you need to leave, I understand. I can see myself home."

He chuckles. "Leda's difficulties aren't so urgent that I would leave you to wander the streets alone so late at night. Monsters roam the city at this hour." A shadow passes over his face, gone in an instant. "I will escort you safely home before I go."

When I go downstairs for breakfast the next morning, Anne is already there. Her gold-and-cream face is wan, bruised purple circles beneath her eyes showing her exhaustion. She holds a cup tight in her hands, but she's staring into the distance, coffee forgotten.

"Good morning." I take a seat across from her at the table. "Long night?"

She blinks several times, focusing on me. "Very."

"Anything you want to talk about?"

"I'm fine."

I purse my lips. She's always trying to protect me. But I don't need her protection, and she needs someone she can talk to. "Hey." Reaching across the table, I take her hand. "I can handle it."

"I said I'm fine, Lucy!" She snatches her hand from mine and shoves her chair back, rising to her feet.

"Okay!" If she doesn't want to talk, I can't force her. But I wish she would open up to me. I'm not the child she thinks I am.

Closing her eyes, she lets out a long breath. Her lips move silently as she counts to ten, a technique she uses whenever she's upset. Then she looks at me. "I need to get some sleep. I'll be working double shifts until this nest is eradicated. Just—" She shakes her head. "Stay out of trouble."

She leaves, and I stare after her. What happened between us? We used to be so close. After Maman and Papa died, all we had was each other. But ever since she found Les Gardiens, her life has revolved around them. She never has time for me anymore. Even when she has a rare free moment, she's distracted, half-listening to whatever I say.

That's what I love about Jakob. When I talk, he listens so intently, it's as though I'm the only one in the room. And he doesn't condescend like Anne does. She treats me like a child, but he talks to me like an equal. Last night, when we were at the museum, he didn't lecture me about the art like Anne would have. Instead, he shared stories about them and asked my thoughts on every piece. When I answered, he nodded, thinking about my response, as though my opinion held great weight.

Thinking of last night leads me to our interrupted dinner, and I frown as I pour myself a cup of coffee. I hope everything is alright. I don't think I like Leda—something about her makes me uncomfortable—but I don't wish her ill, if only because she's Jakob's sister. It seems wrong to wish harm on the family of the man I love. Even if she doesn't seem very familial.

I'm sure I'll know what happened soon enough. Jakob promised we would see each other tonight.

With that happy thought, I take a piece of bread and slather it with butter, putting Leda and her troubles out of my mind.

I meet Jakob on the doorstep that night. His expression is solemn, and my stomach twists with concern for him.

Despite his apparent mood, he draws me into his arms and kisses me deep enough to make me forget my worries.

We don't speak as we walk through the city. There's no need; the understanding between us goes deeper than words. Soon we're strolling along the bank of the Seine. The night is clear, stars twinkling down. In the distance, I can see the Eiffel Tower illuminated by its spotlights. In the other direction, darker but still visible against the sky, are the towers of Notre Dame. A carriage passes us, breaking the silence with the clop of horses' hooves and the rumble of wheels against the cobblestones. The ever-present stench of the city is all but gone tonight, muted by the snow and cold. It's a romantic night, a night in which anything could happen.

We stop on a bridge over the river. As we look out over the water, Jakob pulls me closer to him. He's not warm, the chill of the night seeping into his clothes, but his touch warms me, anyway.

"I must tell you something, Lucille," he says, and his voice is almost wistful.

My heart skips a beat as a million possibilities run through my head, each more ridiculous than the last. Is he going to explain what happened last night with Leda? Or is it unrelated to his family? Maybe he's going to tell me he's secretly betrothed and we can't be together. Or that he's already married.

I shove down my fears. "What is it?"

"I have to return home."

"Oh." It's so innocuous compared to my imaginings, I almost laugh. I turn to look into his eyes. "For how long?"

He's silent, and I frown. "You'll return soon, right?"

He looks past me, out over the city. "It may be years before I can return to Paris."

"What? Why?" I draw back, my frown deepening.

"There are things I cannot tell you. Parts of my life that must be kept in the darkness." He takes my hands. "But I assure you, it is necessity alone that draws me from you."

His eyes are cold and distant. Fear takes root around my heart, and I tighten my grip on his hands. "Are you in danger, Jakob?"

He laughs, though he doesn't seem amused. "No, my dear Lucille. I am not in danger, though I may be if I remain here much longer."

The words crash over me like waves. What could threaten him?

"Is it your sister?" I ask. "Is this about whatever happened last night?"

Storm clouds grow in his eyes. "As I said, there are things in my life I cannot tell you."

Tears spring to my eyes as I feel the distance between us grow. "Will I ever see you again?" I can't imagine living the rest of my life without him.

"I don't know." He stares off. "You cannot know how long I have desired a companion, Lucille. An equal. Someone to walk beside me in this life. When I met you, I thought I had found that companion. It pains me to have to leave you so soon after I found you."

"So don't leave me."

His brow furrows as he refocuses his gaze on me. "But I must leave."

"Take me with you." It's reckless, bordering on absurd, but as soon as the words leave my lips, I know they're right. We're destined to be together, Jakob and I.

"You would come with me?" He scans my face.

I bite my lip and nod, blood pounding in my ears as I wait for his response.

After a beat of silence, he shakes his head, and my heart sinks.

"I cannot allow you to sully yourself in this way," he says. "An unmarried woman traveling alone with a man? It is unthinkable."

Tears threaten to blind me, but I bite my cheek to keep them at bay. Jakob holds my gaze, then sinks down onto one knee.

"I cannot allow you to travel all the way to Alsace alone and unwed with me." He squeezes my hand. "But I would be honored to take you home as my wife. Lucille Allard, will you be my bride?"

My breath leaves me in a rush. "Yes. Yes, of course I will."

The clouds in his eyes vanish, and a warm smile spreads over his face. "My sweet Lucille," he breathes. He draws me down to him, and our lips meet as my knees hit the ground.

He tastes like pomegranate and honey. Our tongues tangle together, his as cool as if he just swallowed a mouthful of snow.

"I need you," he says when he draws back. "Now."

I nod, too breathless to speak.

We end up on my doorstep, though I can't say how we got there. Heat courses through me, and I'm so focused on the touch of Jakob's hand on my back that I can't get the key into the lock. On the third try, the door swings open. I pause, listening for Emile or Anne, but the house is silent.

Upstairs, we slip into my room. I lock the door behind us, and then Jakob is on me.

He tears my coat off me and throws it on the floor. Pinning me to the door with his body, he nips at my neck, hard enough to make me cry out. At the sound, he kisses the spot, running his tongue over it.

"My bride," he whispers into my ear as his hands work to remove my layers of clothing.

Cool air hits my shoulders as he frees me from my shirt, and my heart skips a beat. His bride. He's going to be my husband. I have a sudden need to see his body, and I tug at his coat.

He helps me slip it off, but when I reach for the buttons of his shirt, he shakes his head.

"Sit."

I swallow hard and do as he says, taking a seat on the edge of the bed. The light from the streetlamp outside my window silhouettes him as he unbuttons his shirt.

His body is slim, hinting at muscles, and a spattering of hair dusts his chest. I drink in the sight, my breath quickening as my eyes slide down to the top of his pants. He's like a work of art, and my fingers itch to put him on paper.

Jakob takes a step toward me, but I hold up a hand. "Wait."

He raises a brow but doesn't move as I reach for the sketchbook by my bed. Grabbing a piece of charcoal, I sketch out a hasty outline of his body, then shade in a few details—the shape of his muscles, the curve of his lips as he watches me.

"What are you doing?" Jakob sits on the bed next to me and pulls the sketchbook from my hands.

"I just wanted to remember this." I flush, embarrassment and desire warring for dominance inside my chest. "It's not great, I know, but I'll fix some of the details—"

He silences me with a kiss, pushing me onto my back with the weight of his body.

"It's perfect," he whispers, nipping at my lower lip. It stings, like he broke the skin, but he runs his tongue over the spot, and the pain disappears. "You have an artist's eye."

"Do you think so?" My voice comes out low and breathy.

"I do." He bites the spot where my shoulder meets my neck, teeth bruising my skin in a pleasurable sort of pain. "You're the partner I've always longed for, Lucille. You're everything I've ever wanted."

"Really?" Even though he's asked me to marry him, it's hard to believe that this magnificent man wants me. I reach for him, hoping to pull him tighter to me, but he slides down my body, stopping to press a kiss to my breasts over my stays. When he reaches my legs, he pulls my skirts and undergarments off, baring me to him.

The light in his eyes is hungry, half-crazed with desire, and I want him just as much. I moan his name as he trails soft, cool kisses down my leg.

"Tomorrow," he says. The word is rough with wanting. "We'll marry tomorrow, and once we're home, I'll have you fully."

I whimper. I want him now—need him now—but I can't focus on that for long. He drags a finger through my center, tearing a gasp from my lips.

As I watch, he takes that finger, slick with my desire, and places it in his mouth. His eyes roll back in his head. "Heaven," he murmurs.

I'm trembling with need. "Please," I beg. "Jakob, I need you."

His eyes meet mine, the expression almost predatory. An instant later, I'm on my stomach. His body presses me into the quilts, lips at my ear.

"I need you more," he whispers. Gripping me by the neck with one hand, he uses his other hand to thrust two fingers into my center.

The sudden intrusion startles a cry from me, and I bury my face in the pillow to muffle it. I know Emile can't hear from his apartment, and Anne is supposed to be gone, but I don't want to risk being caught. I'd die from wanting if someone interrupted us.

As Jakob works his fingers in and out, he kisses down my back. Shivering, I grind against him. I need more—more speed, more pressure, more...something. I don't know what I need, but Jakob does. His thumb finds the nub between my legs and circles it, and I bite the pillow to keep from begging him to end the agonizing bliss.

He kisses the soft skin of my bottom, then bites it, harder than before, as my climax overtakes me. I can't see, can't hear, can't even breathe. There's nothing but the stars winking behind my eyes and the inexorable movements of his fingers inside me, the pull of his mouth on my skin.

My body goes boneless, and Jakob withdraws his hand. He presses a kiss to the spot where he'd bit me, then gently rolls me over onto my back.

"My sweet Lucille," he whispers, and he kisses my lips. He tastes tangy, almost coppery, and I wonder if it's my arousal on his tongue. There's a fog of exhaustion threatening to drag me under. "Tomorrow, you'll be mine."

Chapter

5

In the morning, I find a note from Anne on the breakfast table. She's staying at the headquarters of Les Gardiens and won't be home for a few days. I don't know if I'm disappointed or relieved that I won't see her before I leave. With Anne, I'm a terrible liar, and I know that if she found out about Jakob, she'd lock me up and refuse to let me leave. It's time for me to set out on my own, but I can't help wishing I could give her a proper goodbye.

Instead, I sit down and write out a lengthy letter explaining everything. How Jakob and I met, our courtship, our hasty engagement. I tell her I'm sorry for keeping things from her, and I promise she can come visit as soon as we're settled.

My belongings are already packed in a trunk waiting by the door, and as darkness falls, a knock announces Jakob's arrival.

A carriage waits on the street. The driver takes my trunk and loads it onto the carriage as I turn and bid goodbye to my childhood home.

Tears clog my throat. How long will it be before I return? Years, perhaps. And Emile—I didn't even tell him farewell.. I spent most of the day in my room packing, and I was too nervous to eat supper this evening. He'll be in bed now, and when he discovers my letter to Anne in the morning, he'll be angry with me, and confused.

Maybe I should wake him and ex-plain things.

"Come, my love." Jakob's voice beckons from inside the carriage.

I shake myself and turn away from the house. I'll write to Emile from my new home, and when Anne comes to visit, he can join us.

I can't remain here while my destiny waits.

With a deep breath, I allow the driver to help me into the carriage, where Jakob sits in the silence.

We're both silent as the carriage begins moving. I wonder what he's thinking. Is he as nervous as I am? I feel as though my heart is going to pound out of my chest. It's too dark to see his expression, and I can't even hear his breathing over the sound of the carriage wheels on the road. If I hadn't seen him as I climbed in, I'd think I was alone.

Too soon and not soon enough, the carriage stops. The driver opens the door for us, and Jakob climbs out, offering a hand to help me alight.

"One last chance to run," he murmurs, brushing my cheek with his chilled hand. I tremble, and he smiles, showing me his teeth.

This isn't the wedding I always dreamed of. I'd hoped for a white dress and a church filled with all our friends and family. Instead, I'm wearing a light blue traveling gown, traveling through the night for an anonymous ceremony with none of my loved ones in attendance.

But the wedding itself doesn't matter—the lifetime after does. And Jakob is my destiny. "I won't run from you," I say.

His smile widens. "Then let us go."

He takes a lantern from the driver and leads me into an inconspicuous, unlit building.

"Watch your step," he cautions as we descend a set of winding stone stairs. The air is colder here, the room—impossibly—darker. My breath quickens the further down we go. We're underground now, though I can't tell how far down.

The stairs end in a tunnel, and we follow it. The walls are gray stone, like the stairs. A heavy feeling in the air makes my skin crawl. I cling to Jakob's arm, too tense to speak. Is this the venue he's arranged for our wedding?

At last, the tunnel widens. Ahead of us, Jakob's family waits in flickering candlelight.

Leda steps forward and takes my hand. "My congratulations, sister. Welcome to the family." There's an ironic undertone to her words. Her smile is chilling, and there's a hatred in her eyes directed at me. I swallow and try to pull away, but she tightens her grip as her smile widens. "I'm ever so pleased that dear Jakob has found a companion."

I look over at Jakob, but he's oblivious, talking to Aeron in low tones. "Thank you," I say to Leda, trying to ignore my racing heart. "I'm...excited."

Jakob slips an arm around my waist. "Stop monopolizing my bride, Leda."

The hatred melts from her expression. "Merely offering my congratulations, dear brother." She squeezes my hand a little too tight and releases it.

Aeron gestures for us to stand before him. "Time runs short," he says.

We take our places. Leda stands next to Aeron, the two of them bracketed by enormous iron candelabras. Jakob nods at his father. "We're ready."

"It is an honor and a privilege," Aeron begins, "to join my son Jakob to the companion he has so longed for."

The rush of blood in my ears makes it hard to focus on the words. Excitement and anxiety course through me, and I look around the room, hoping to find something to calm myself. The stones that make up the walls have a strange shape, forming a curious pattern. I frown, squinting to see better.

They're bones.

My blood runs cold. I know where we are. We're in an ossuary, in a room beneath the city built to house the dead. Anne told me about these catacombs. She calls them a breeding ground for evil. Creatures of the night congregate in these tunnels, and woe to the innocent who wander in unawares.

Does Jakob know the dangers here? Do Leda and Aeron? Have I stumbled into the midst of a nest of demons?

No, Jakob is no danger to me. He cares for me, protects me. Our souls are bound by fate.

I steal a glance at him. He's watching his father, but he feels my gaze and looks over with a smile. Comforted, I return my attention to Aeron.

"We are here in this most holy of places— for what could be more holy than the eternal resting place of thousands of souls?—to join for eternity these two."

Leda's smile has gone brittle, almost a grimace, and her eyes are fixed on Jakob. I take a step closer to him. I don't know what claim she thinks she has on him, but he's mine. I watch her with narrowed eyes, and when Aeron reaches the vows, I repeat after him, hardly hearing the words. The cold press of Jakob's touch grounds me.

Then the ceremony is over. As Aeron pronounces us man and wife, Jakob takes my face in his hands and gives me a gentle kiss.

A moment later, it seems, we're bundled back into the carriage. Jakob bids goodbye to his father and sister, then closes the door behind us. We're alone, ensconced in darkness and the sweet smell of cedar.

"Sleep, Lucille," he says as the carriage lurches to a start. "We have a long journey ahead of us."

Sleep? Energy courses through me, leaving sleep an impossibility. I'm alone with my husband for the first time. How could I sleep?

I open my mouth to tell him I'm not tired, but a yawn comes out instead. A strange lethargy settles over me. Jakob tucks me into his arms, covering us both with a blanket from the carriage seat and presses a kiss to my head. "Sleep," he says again. "You will not be harmed."

Chapter 6

I wake with a jolt. Looking around the room, I don't recognize my surroundings. I'm in a well-furnished room, lying in a curtained four-poster bed. The fire in the grate burns hot, filling the room with light and driving away the winter chill.

There's a knock at the door, and Jakob enters the room. "Ah, you are awake."

"Have we stopped at an inn?" I ask, slipping out from beneath the covers. I'm dressed in my white cotton nightgown, and my dressing robe hangs over the arm of a nearby chair.

"We are home, Lucille." Jakob frowns. "Do you not remember?"

Home? I'd thought we would travel for days. How could we be here already? "Of course," I say, not wanting to seem foolish. "I'm sorry. I must have been more tired than I thought."

He smiles, and the sight sends warmth rushing through me. "You must dress." He picks up my robe and holds it out for me. "I am eager to show you our home."

His gaze is heavy-lidded as he helps me into my robe. He ties it in the front, and his hand brushes my breast. I shiver, lips parting, but Jakob takes a step back and smiles.

In the boudoir adjoining my bedroom, I find my clothes already unpacked, my violet tea gown pressed and hanging from the dressing screen. How long have we been here? I feel disoriented. Blurry images fill my mind, the rocking of the carriage and the sound of wheels on the road, the murmur of voices as Jakob spoke to our driver. I have a vague impression in my mind of a large manor, silhouetted black against the moonlit sky.

I shake my head to clear it. How did I forget the journey? But of course it happened. We're here, after all. Alsace. My new home.

I dress quickly, then clean my teeth and pin my hair atop my head. Looking at my image in the mirror, I wish for a pot of rouge to add color to my sallow-looking cheeks. But that will have to wait. I don't want to keep my husband waiting.

"Are you ready?"

Jakob's voice comes from behind me, and I whirl, heart in my throat. I was so focused on my appearance I didn't see him approach in the mirror.

"I am." I smooth my skirts to compose myself. My mind feels fragmented, chaotic. The days of travel have worn on me. I hope the sensation will fade as I adjust to my surroundings.

"This house has belonged to my family for centuries. I've done my best to improve it, but I hope you'll make your own mark as mistress of the house."

Mistress of the house. The phrase sends a thrill through me. I'm married. This is my home. I'd lost sight of that in the confusion after waking, but Jakob is my husband now.

A thought interrupts my happiness, and I stiffen. Have we consummated the marriage yet?

I rifle through the blurry memories of our journey. No, we didn't. I might have forgotten the finer details, but I wouldn't forget that. Jakob offers me his arm, and I take it, heat rushing to my center. Now that we're home, we'll have all the time in the world to enjoy each other's bodies.

He leads me through a side door into a bedroom that adjoins my own. The bed appears untouched, and the fireplace is cold. There's no window, the only light coming from a single oil lamp next to the bed, and the cold and darkness lend a gloomy air to the room. "This is my room," he says.

I walk toward the bed, trailing my fingers over the covers. They're luxurious, made of the finest fabric. Mahogany curtains hang around the dark wood bedframe. "It's lovely."

"It's lonely," Jakob replies. "I hope to spend less time here, now that you've arrived."

I flush at the implication of his words. Suddenly the darkness doesn't feel gloomy; it feels alluring. Jakob's gaze lingers on my lips, and for a moment, all I can hear is the sound of my breathing and the pounding of my heart.

"I'd like that."

The words are barely a whisper, but he hears me. He takes a step closer, so I have to look up to see his face. "Would you?"

Heat pools low in my stomach as I nod.

"I'd meant to wait," he murmurs. "Meant to give you a few hours to adjust to your surroundings. But now that I have you here…"

"I don't want to wait."

"I don't either." He runs his thumb along my bottom lip. "Seeing you in that nightdress was torture."

I don't respond. I'm too focused on the way his other hand is tracing the curve of my body.

"You were temptation in your nightdress," he goes on, "but in this? You're delectable." He leans in to kiss me.

This kiss is less gentle than ones we've shared before. Our tongues and teeth clash against one another. I taste the coppery tang of blood—his or mine, I don't know—but Jakob doesn't stop. He walks me backward until I fall onto the bed, then he climbs on top of me.

"My sweet Lucille." He grinds himself into my center. "Tell me you want me."

"I do." I cling to him, fingers digging into the fabric of his shirt. "I need you, Jakob."

The sound he makes is inhuman as he takes the top of my dress in his hands. I hear a ripping sound, and my breasts are free, the dress in pieces.

He leans down and takes one nipple into his mouth, swirling his tongue around. Then he bites my breast, so hard that I think he must have pierced the skin. An instant later, the pain fades, and my whole body thrums with desire.

I quiver with need. "Please, Jakob." If he doesn't take me now, I'll go mad.

Without removing his mouth from my breast, he sheds his pants and lines himself with my opening. Slowly, he pushes inside, and I spread my legs wide to ease his entrance. It burns like ice, pain and pleasure melding together.

He lifts his head from my breast and licks the spot he bit. "Exquisite," he whispers.

"More," I beg, my eyes shut tight, and he obliges, sinking into me until he's fully seated. The sensation is rapturous death.

I need to feel him move, but he remains still. Jerking my hips, I try to urge him toward what I want. Instead, he puts a hand around my throat—not squeezing, just holding me. My eyes fly open.

"You're mine." He drags himself out and thrusts back in. "Forever."

"Yours," I pant in agreement.

Bending his head back down, he bites my other breast, and I feel the same sharp pain, followed by the rush of warmth and need. I throw my head back with a cry, clinging so tight to Jakob that I fear I'll draw blood. My enthusiasm urges him on, and he increases the pace of his thrusts.

It could be minutes or hours before my pleasure reaches a crescendo and my climax crashes over me. A moment later, Jakob follows, his whole body shuddering with the force.

He removes his teeth from my breast, licking and kissing the wound. I'll be bruised tomorrow, I'm certain, but the thought of Jakob leaving his claim on me doesn't bother me. I'll be proud to wear the marks of his lovemaking, even if no one can see.

Jakob goes to his washbasin and returns a moment later with a wet cloth, which he uses to clean between my legs. I watch him, too tired to move beneath his ministrations. After returning the cloth to the basin, he climbs into bed with me, pulling a blanket atop us.

His body is cool as ever, and I shiver, grateful for the added warmth.

"Is it always like this?" I murmur into his chest.

"Like what?"

I can't keep my eyes open. "Exhausting."

He laughs, the low sound rumbling through me. "No, sweet Lucille. No, it's not."

My response comes out garbled, and he laughs again. "Sleep, my bride. We can talk later."

I'm more lucid when I wake later that day— or night? I still haven't seen a clock. Looking around, I see I haven't been moved from Jakob's bedroom, though a fire has been lit now. He sits by the hearth, a small yellow book in hand and an amused smile on his face.

"What are you reading?"

He looks up, his expression softening as his eyes meet mine. "A tale by an Irishman obsessed with the macabre. How do you feel?"

I sit up, the blanket falling away from my naked body, and take stock of myself. I'm groggy, and my core is sore. Other than that, I feel good. Better than good. "Wonderful,"

I say, rising and walking to him. His eyes darken as he watches me approach, taking in my naked flesh. An answering desire floods low in my abdomen, and though I know I'm not ready for him to take me again, I almost wish he would.

Jakob knows what I need better than I do, though. "You need to eat." He reaches for the robe draped over the back of his chair and helps me into it. "And I believe I promised you a tour."

He waits while I dress, then leads me out of the room and through the halls. It's enormous, and I don't know how I'll ever remember my way around. Hopefully the servants will direct me if I get lost.

The house is filled to the brim with works of art and historical artifacts. It's like walking through a museum, and I don't know where to look first. Jakob shows me illuminated manuscripts from the Far East, sculptures from ancient Greece and Rome, paintings by the Renaissance masters... There are no windows in the house—to protect the precious art from sunlight, he explains—but he's had electric lighting installed to illuminate the halls.

We eat a roast dinner in the dining hall, surrounded by painted silk tapestries, and talk about the history of the art he's collected. He owns art from every place he's ever visited, and I hang on every word of his descriptions.

"I would love to see it," I say as he finishes telling me about the Colosseum in Rome, the ancient theater where gladiators once battled.

"Perhaps we will go one day." He smiles, then his expression grows solemn. "There is still one part of the house we have not discussed, and it is perhaps the most important room of all."

He takes my hand, his touch as cold as ever, and leads me through the halls to a winding, shadowy staircase.

"You are my bride," he says as we climb the steps, "and the one I trust above all others. No one may enter this room for any reason. Not even you."

My curiosity rises as we reach the landing. What is the purpose of a room no one can enter? There's a faint, musty smell in the air here, and my skin prickles, sensing an unseen threat.

Jakob slips a hand into his pocket and draws out a small bronze key. "Behind this door lies the secret to my destruction. I must ask—no, beg you not to open it. But because of my great love for you, I give you the key." He places it in my hands and wraps my fingers around it. "You have the key to my downfall, my sweet Lucille. Guard it well."

"I will." My chest tightens. How much faith must he have in me to give me this?

As we descend the stairs, I glance back at the unassuming door. I can't deny I'm curious, and my fingers itch to open it. But I trust Jakob. I can't harm him.

The room and its contents will have to remain a mystery.

Chapter 7

We spend the next week at home, settling in. Jakob keeps late hours, not rising until almost sunset and staying awake until the early hours of the morning. It's a familiar sschedule for me, so I do the same. We spend almost all our waking hours together, reading books and discussing plays. Every night, we take a walk through the snow-covered gardens, admiring how the moonlight reflects on the frozen landscape.

When I'm not with Jakob, I entertain myself by painting my surroundings. Tonight he has business in the nearby town, so I'm working in the kitchen, recording the bustle of the servants as they prepare our dinner for Jakob's return.

I sit in a corner with my canvas and easel, a palette of oranges and browns in one hand, and a brush in the other. As I form the outline of the wood-burning stove, the cook, a slender, elderly woman, steps around me with a large pot of water in her hands.

"I hope I'm not in the way," I say. "I can leave, or move."

"It's no trouble." She places the pot on the stove and turns back to me. "It's a pleasure to have you here. The herr is often gone, and even when he is here, there's no…" She pauses, thinking for a moment, and then shrugs. "There is no life here without a mistress of the house. When his last wife was—"

Cold shock suffuses my body, and I cut her off. "Last wife?"

Her shoulders stiffen, and she glances at me over her shoulder. "Forgive me. I spoke out of turn."

"No, go on." My chest is tight, the room swimming around me. What happened to Jakob's wife? Why would he keep this from me? Is he still in love with her?

My mind goes back to the locked room upstairs. Maybe that's the secret he's hiding behind the door. A shrine to his dead wife, or proof of bigamy. Or even the wife herself, a madwoman locked inside the tower, visited on the rarest of occasions.

"It's not my place to say." She shakes her head. "Anyway, it was a long time ago."

No matter how much I press, she won't say anything else on the matter. Conceding defeat, I pack up my paints and head to my room.

Dinner is a hearty potato soup with warm, crusty bread, but I can't bring myself to take a bite. My stomach is tight, and I watch as Jakob eats, oblivious to my despair.

"You are quiet tonight, my bride," he says as he mops up the last drops of soup with the crust of his bread. "Is the food not to your liking?"

I pick up my spoon, intending to take a bite, then drop it into the bowl with a clatter. I have to know. "Were you married before me?"

"Ah." He wipes his mouth with his napkin and sets it aside. "You have spoken with the servants."

A tight fist squeezes my heart. "Why didn't you tell me?"

"It is…a painful subject for me." He looks past me, eyes going glassy. "It was long ago, but the pain has not dissipated over time."

"Who was she?" I dig my nails into my palm to keep from crying. He's still in love with her; I can see it in his eyes.

He focuses on me again. "Her name was Marie. Like you, she was a young French woman with golden hair and eyes full of wonder. We married young—I was new to this life and new to my wealth, and Marie was eager to leave her world behind."

"What happened?" The words are almost a whisper, but I have to know.

"She betrayed me."

I don't speak as Jakob stands and walks across the room toward me. He holds out his hand to help me to my feet.

"She was pregnant," he says, his voice low. "The pregnancy changed her. She grew distant, suspicious. She would fly into fits, lock herself in her bedroom, and refuse to eat."

I'm hardly breathing. Jakob isn't either. We're standing inches apart, but the air between us is frigid and taut. He's staring straight into my soul, our eyes locked together.

"Then she tried to kill me. There was a struggle, and…" He looks away. "She died."

My breath leaves me in a rush. "I'm so sorry, Jakob." I place a hand on his chest. "I didn't know." It seems foolish now, my fear, anger, and jealousy. She's dead—long dead. There's no sense in envying a dead woman.

He takes my hand in his and presses a kiss to it. "Forgive me for not telling you, my sweet Lucille. I don't like to dwell on it."

"There's nothing to forgive," I say, and I draw him to me for a kiss.

The fire pops in the grate, light dancing over Jakob's hair. It's almost impossible to capture him in color, but I'm doing my best, alternating tiny brushstrokes of coal-black, sapphire blue, and brilliant orange in the painting before me.

He's absorbed in his book, the same one he's been reading since we arrived home. He's read a few passages aloud to me, silly romantic things. One of the characters is called Lucy, and he takes great delight in detailing the romantic accomplishments of the young woman who shares my name. All the men in the story are fighting to marry her, though she seems to be both flighty and frail.

He finishes the book as I paint. Setting it aside, he looks up at me. "How goes your painting?"

I turn the canvas around to show him.

"Marvelous," he says. "You are a master."

Flushing at the praise, I duck my head. "It's far from finished."

"And yet it is already a magnificent piece of art."

"I have a good subject."

He reaches out to take my hand. "I shall have to commission a painting of you, as well."

My blush deepens.

"It's late." He rises and pulls me to my feet. "We should retire."

Glancing at my pocketwatch, I see he's right. It's well past dawn, though the lack of windows in the house makes our days and nights feel timeless, like a dream.

I set my palette aside. "I can finish the painting tomorrow."

"Unfortunately not," Jakob says as he leads me upstairs. "A matter of business requires my attention out of town. I have to leave tomorrow evening."

"Oh." It shouldn't be a surprise. Surely I didn't expect him to be home all the time? But I had hoped our honeymoon would last longer than a week. "How long will you be gone?"

"No more than two or three days." He stops at the top of the stairs and looks into my eyes. "It will pain me to leave you, my dear Lucille. I will return as soon as I can."

That mollifies me. At least he's as reluctant to leave me as I am to have him go. "Could I go with you?" He did promise to show me the world, after all. Why not start close to home?

He smiles. "While I look forward to traveling with you, you cannot come this time. It will be a short journey, and there won't be time for sightseeing."

I fight the urge to pout like a spoiled child. He won't be gone long. In the mean time, I can use his absence as an opportunity to adjust to being mistress of the house. I've been so absorbed in him, I haven't had time to learn much about running a household of this size.

I bid him farewell the next night after supper, waving as his carriage drives down the road in the gray post-sunset light. Once he disappears around the bend, I turn and go back inside, already missing him.

DAKOTAH GUMM

For the first few hours, I explore
the house, familiarizing myself with the
rooms Jakob and I have spent the least
amount of time in.

Near midnight, I stand at the bottom of
a narrow staircase, my gaze drawn upward.
What could Jakob be hiding in that room?
Proof of some illegal activity? A weapon? A
grim secret from his past?

It occurs to me how little I know of my
husband. How did he meet his first wife? Who
was his mother? Where did he get his wealth,
since his father still lives? Why does he look
so different from the rest of his family? I don't
even know how old he is.

The key, resting on a chain around my
neck, tingles against my skin, and I clench
it in my fist. Taking a cautious step onto the
stairs, I hold my breath and look around.
Jakob is gone, and none of the servants are
nearby. I'm unobserved. Nothing is stopping
me from opening the door.

I long to open the door, to unlock all of
my husband's secrets until there's nothing left
between us. It's not mistrust that urges me up
the stairs; it's a desire to know him better.

My heart pounds in my ears as I reach
the landing. The edges of the key bite

into my palm, and I take the chain from around my neck.

Can I break the trust he's placed in me?

I stop with my hand inches from the lock. I can't betray him. Not like this. I want to learn about Jakob, but I want him to share his secrets with me because he trusts me. Not because I've stolen them from him.

Replacing the key around my neck, I let out a long breath. For tonight, his secrets will have to wait.

Chapter

It's mid-afternoon when I rise the next day. Jakob's absence has left me off-kilter, and I don't know what to do with myself. Once I've dressed and eaten, I go to the library and browse the countless shelves. None of the priceless manuscripts draw my attention, but I catch sight of the small novel Jakob was reading.

The cover reads "Dracula, by Bram Stoker." It's a ridiculous story, according to my husband, but maybe the shared experience of reading it will draw us closer together. If nothing else, it can distract me from the emptiness of the enormous house.

I'm only a few pages into the book when a footman knocks at the door. "There is a woman here to see you."

I look up, brows raised. I haven't made friends here yet; I've been too occupied with Jakob to enter the local society. And the hour is late for social calls. Who could it be?

"I'll see her," I say, curiosity drawing me from my comfortable seat by the library fire.

In the foyer, a woman in black trousers and a worn coat waits, looking around the room. She seems out of place, better suited to the nighttime streets of Paris than to our ornate entrance hall, but my heart leaps as I see her.

"Anne!" I run to her. She meets me halfway, clutching me in a tight embrace. The hard edges of her crucifix dig into my chest, and I pull back to smile at her.

"Lucy, thank God." She looks me over. "He hasn't hurt you. You're alive."

I laugh out loud at that. "No, he hasn't hurt me! Jakob is my husband." I clasp her hands in mine. "I'm sorry I left without talking to you, but it was all so sudden. We met weeks ago. I wanted to tell you—" I break off, a twinge of guilt eating at me. "I knew you wouldn't approve. But he had to leave Paris, and I couldn't be without him. We're in love. We're married now. We're happy! I want you to be happy for me."

She scowls, her face settling into its usual expression of disapproval and worry. "You barely know him, Lucy. He's not who you think he is."

"What do you mean?" My smile falters a little. "You've never even met him."

"I don't have to. I know his type. I've hunted them for years. I know it's hard to hear, Lucy, but your 'husband,'" she spits the word out, "isn't human."

I let out a brittle laugh, pulling away. "What? Of course he is." Her work has made her paranoid, seeing monsters in ordinary people. "I understand you want to protect me, Anne, but Jakob isn't—"

"Have you ever seen him in the daylight?" she snaps, cutting me off. "Ever seen his reflection? Ever seen the bed he sleeps in?"

"I—" I want to tell her she's wrong… but she's not. Even since we married, I've not seen him in the direct sunlight. The house is clear of reflective surfaces, aside from the small mirror in my boudoir, so I've never seen his image in a mirror. And while I've seen his bed, it's never been ruffled as if from sleep. It's always fresh. Unused.

"You've been unusually tired, haven't you? Dizzy? Cold?"

I frown. I hadn't given it much thought, but I have been feeling ill. Especially after we make love.

Noting my hesitation, she presses on. "He's a vampire, Lucy. And judging by the way you look, he's been feeding on you. The nest I was tracking before you left? It was his. We caught one of them. He told us everything, all about the rest of his nest. About his spawn, Jakob, who left the city just before we closed in on them." She looks deep into my eyes, her expression more earnest than ever. "About you, the golden-haired young bride his 'son' was taking with him."

My chest tightens. Aeron. Leda. Jakob. Can they be the nest Anne was tracking? Jakob warned me about himself. He told me not to trust him. He told me Paris was dangerous for him. What could be more dangerous to a vampire than Les Gardiens?

But even if he is one of the undead, that changes nothing. The love between us is real. I know it is. He might have hidden this from me, but that doesn't mean he doesn't care for me. After all, he gave me the key to his destruction.

I touch the key that hangs from my neck. What hides behind that door? Is it a weapon? A way to end him? Or is it evidence of what he is?

"I can't believe it." I shake my head, taking a step back. "Not without proof."

Anne throws her hands up in the air. "What more proof do you need? Is my word not enough?"

I twist the key in my hands. Can I do this? Can I betray him?

What if Anne is wrong?

I have to know. "Come with me," I say.

I lead her through the long, dark halls, then up the stairs into the tower. The air is dry and frigid, and the smell of dust and sweet incense linger around us.

I stop at the landing and turn to Anne, holding up the key. "Jakob gave me this. He told me whatever is behind this door can destroy him. If he's..." I swallow hard. "If he is what you say he is, there's proof inside this room."

She nods, brow furrowed, and steps back so I can open the door.

My hands tremble as I lift the key to the lock. I can feel the blood rushing through me.

My breathing sounds too loud in the quiet staircase.

The key slides into the lock and turns with a loud click. I hold my breath as I step inside and look around. My heart stops.

Corpses line the walls.

There are dozens of them, all dried husks. Their dresses are old, though perfectly preserved. Some wear headdresses in styles that haven't been seen since the Renaissance. Others have golden hair flowing loose over their shoulders.

I tremble as I look around the room. Is this what Jakob has planned for me? Once I've outlived my usefulness to him, does he intend to turn me into one of these trophies?

Anne follows me into the room, and I hear her sharp intake of breath. "Are these his…."

Wives. It's all the wives that came before me. Is Marie, the wife he told me about, in here? Was she the first, or the latest? Did she discover his secret and try to kill him?

Nausea roils my stomach, but it's not my surroundings that upset me. It's not even the idea of becoming part of Jakob's collection. It's the thought that he didn't intend to keep me. He didn't want me to be his eternal companion. He didn't mean for our marriage to last forever.

"I've never seen anything like this," Anne says. She leans in to examine a woman in a black dress with a high-ruffed white collar. "Some of the creatures keep trophies, but I've never found a room full of mummified victims before. This is sickening."

It should be sickening, but there's a grim sort of beauty to the scene. He's arranged each woman artfully, as though she stopped for a moment of rest and never got up. I can see them all as they would have been in life, stunning and spirited. They sit in a semicircle around a curtained window, facing each other, as though deep in conversation about art and culture. We have a camaraderie, these women and me, and it goes beyond our shared husband. I see in their faces that same lust for adventure.

The wife nearest to me wears a green taffeta dress a decade or so out of style. She must be the most recent addition. Did she find the room as well? Did it terrify her, or did it sadden her, like it does me? Did she hope to be his eternal companion?

"You couldn't resist, could you?"

Jakob's voice comes from behind me, and I whirl, heart in my throat. He's standing in the doorway, his brows drawn together with disappointment.

"I'm sorry," I step toward him, but Anne stops me with a hand on my arm.

"Don't apologize," she snaps. "You have nothing to apologize for. He's a monster."

"They never can help themselves." He ignores Anne, glancing around at the bodies on display. "No matter how I warn them, they always come into the room." His gaze returns to me. "I thought you were different, Lucille. Hoped you were different."

"She knows what you are now." My sister moves in front of me, drawing the stake from her belt. "You don't hold any power over her."

If only that was true. I should be terrified, but the same pull that drew us together still holds sway. "What if I had been different, Jakob? What if I'd stayed out? Would you have kept your secret forever?"

"Stop engaging with him, Lucy," Anne says. "You can't reason with these creatures. You're nothing but a meal to them."

Tears blur my sight, but I don't remove my eyes from Jakob's. "Was that all this was to you? Did you marry me just so I would be here for you to feed on?"

He takes a step closer, opening his mouth as if to speak, but Anne holds the stake out before her. "Don't touch her!"

"I meant what I said, Lucille." He ignores her, though he stays out of reach. "I have desired a companion for longer than you can imagine. Someone to share my eternity with. Someone with my same taste for beauty, the same outlook on the world. Aeron and Leda, they have no finesse. Aeron may have sired me, but I cannot spend the rest of my existence in his nest. I need someone who understands me."

He circles us, and we turn to keep him in sight—me because I can't bear to look away, Anne because she's waiting for a lapse in his guard.

"For centuries I've claimed brides like you." He waves a hand around, indicating the bodies surrounding us. "Innocent, trusting women with no one to protect them. I gave them the key and left them alone in my home. At the first opportunity, they opened the door, and their affection turned to fear.

"But you..." He looks into my eyes. "You were different. I warned you away from me, and you kept coming back. When I left you alone with the key, I thought you might leave the room untouched. I began to think you

94

could be my companion. My true companion. My equal."

He sighs, stopping by one of the bodies
and running a hand through its long yellow
hair. "But I return to find you here."

"I trust you!" I cry, tears spilling out
over my cheeks. "I trusted you. I didn't want
to come in."

"And yet you did." He's impassive, a cool
contrast to my breaking heart. "I wanted to
make you like me. Instead I must add you and
your sister to my collection."

"You can try, demon," Anne snarls. She
lunges forward, stake aimed for his heart. He
sidesteps, dodging her blow.

"Don't!" I cry. I grab at her arm, trying to
hold her back. I can't bear to see her hurt him.
Even if he plans to kill us. I don't want to live
in a world where he doesn't exist.

"He's not real!" she says. "Whatever you
thought you had with him is imagined, Lucy.
He wants to kill you."

"Then let him!" My face is soaked with
tears. "Better death than life without him."

She shakes me off, knocking me to the
ground. I hit the floor with a thud, wood
splinters slicing my hands.

"You've destroyed her mind!" Anne dives at Jakob. Rage twists her features, but I barely see it. My whole being is focused on Jakob. She's going to kill him. She's one of Les Gardiens, the most elite fighting force the world has ever seen. He doesn't stand a chance against her.

The world slows around me. I scramble to my feet as her stake slices through the air. He sees it, but he can't move fast enough. His eyes widen in shock, hands moving out before him.

I thrust myself between them just in time. The wooden stake pierces the tender flesh where my neck and shoulder meet. Warm blood gushes from the wound, soaking my dress.

Anne stumbles back as I sway. She looks down at the stake in her hands, now coated with my blood. Her eyes go wide with horror.

Jakob catches me as I fall to the floor. "What have you done, my Lucille?" He brushes the hair from my face, cradling me in his arms.

"I couldn't let her kill you, Jakob." I'm cold, the world going gray as my lifeblood leaves me. "I promised you eternity. I can't imagine living without you."

"Living?" he says, echoing the words of the play we saw the night we met. "Our servants will do that for us." He bites his wrist, tearing the skin, and presses the wound to my mouth. I lap up the blood, salt and copper sliding down my throat. As I drink, he sinks his teeth into my wound, the sting of the bite layering on top of the existing pain. Then he lifts me into the air.

Anne doesn't move, frozen in shock where she stands pressed against the wall. I can feel my transformation beginning, Jakob's venom coursing through my veins, as he strides across the room. My heartbeat slows, the skin around my wound knits back together, and strength returns to my body. I wrap my arms around Jakob's neck as, one-handed, he pushes the curtain aside and opens the window. The sky outside is dark, and evening air caresses my skin.

He looks into my eyes, affection softening the stony features of his face. "Come, my love," he says, his voice soft. "Let us begin our eternity."

He leaps from the windowsill. Wind rushes past as the ground rises to greet us. A moment before we crash, wings burst from his back, shredding his shirt, and we lift into the air. The moon illuminates our ascent, casting a silvery light over the scene. My heart beats once, twice, three times…and then falls silent, never to beat again.

I take a deep breath with my new, undead lungs, and tighten my grip around my husband's neck. Fangs descend in my mouth. I smile up at him, showing my teeth.

"Forever," I say.

"Forever," he agrees. He bends his head down to meet mine, and our lips meet in a promise of eternity.

Epilogue

Anne

I stare out the window at their retreating silhouettes. My hands are spattered with Lucy's blood. It's cold. Sticky.

I killed her. I killed my sister.

Her body's still moving—I can see it in the distance, cradled in the arms of her inhuman husband—but it's not her anymore. That thing living inside her is a demon. Lucy's soul, my sister's soul, is dead and gone.

The logical part of me, my Gardien training, says it's not my fault. She went with him willingly. His beautiful facade blinded her to the rot beneath. But don't I hold the blame for her eagerness to leave? I sheltered her too much. I thought I was keeping her safe, but I was keeping her naive. Too naive, too trusting, to see the danger when it came for her.

I stand in silent vigil as the last gray hints of daylight fade to black and the stars come out. When I finally turn away from the window, my eyes are as dry as the blood that's now flaking off my fingers.

I'm too late to save Lucy, but I can fix this. The blue-bearded monster and his new undead bride have to be destroyed.

My first task is to resign from Les Gardiens. I can't be a protector of Paris if I can't even protect my sister. Next, I have to warn the inhabitants of this house and the nearby town. They don't know the evil they've been harboring. It's time they learned the danger they're in.

Then the hunt can begin.

Acknowledgments

First and foremost, I have to thank my family. I hope you never read this, but thank you for believing in me. Andrew, you've been my biggest supporter since I started on this crazy career path. Kids, your love keeps me going when I want to give up. Mom and Dad, you taught me to read and follow my dreams, and more importantly, you raised me to have faith in the Creator, Redeemer, and Comforter who sustains me through all things.

Delanie, I'm forever grateful that you were my first reader. Obviously, you're my favorite sibling. Dyami and Dalton, you won't read this, so it doesn't matter what I say to you. I'd say you were adopted, but that would imply you were wanted. (If you want a good acknowledgment, you'll have to actually read my books.)

Next, to the woman who made this book happen, Harmony Marquardt: I'm like a little trash goblin, hammering my pieces of scrap metal into something resembling a shape. Without you standing over my shoulder to give direction and polish my creation, it would never be the beautiful thing it is today. You're the best friend I never met.

A special thanks to all my early readers, especially Zara J. Black, Amélia Cognet, Marie Still, Laurae Knight, Elizabeth Myrva,

K.L. Mielke, Courtney Taylor, and Heather Carter. Your feedback was invaluable, and your hilarious (and often inappropriate) commentary turned editing into a joy. I also want to thank Write Like a Mother, Moms Who Write, Project X, and the other online communities I'm in, without whom I would still be stumbling around in the dark, trying to turn words into books.

Finally, thank you, dear reader, for taking a chance on this story. I hope you found something in it worth keeping. May we share many pages to come.

www.ingramcontent.com/pod-product-compliance
Lightning Source LLC
Chambersburg PA
CBHW031546310726
48971CB00008B/2653